ALSO BY CHRISTINE MCDONNELL

It's a Deal, Dog Boy
Toad Food and Measle Soup

Ballet Bug

Ballet Bug

BY
CHRISTINE MCDONNELL

ILLUSTRATED BY
MARTHA DOTY

VIKING

Martha would like to thank Janet and Bernadette of Portfolio Solutions for their tireless support. She would also like to thank Studio B Dance Center in Eastchester, N.Y., for their help in researching for this project.

VIKING
Published by the Penguin Group
Penguin Putnam Books for Young Readers,
345 Hudson Street, New York, New York 10014, U.S.A.
Penguin Books Ltd, 27 Wrights Lane, London W8 5TZ, England
Penguin Books Australia Ltd, Ringwood, Victoria, Australia
Penguin Books Canada Ltd, 10 Alcorn Avenue, Toronto, Ontario, Canada M4V 3B2
Penguin Books (N.Z.) Ltd, 182-190 Wairau Road, Auckland 10, New Zealand

Penguin Books Ltd, Registered Offices: Harmondsworth, Middlesex, England

First published in 2001 by Viking,
a division of Penguin Putnam Books for Young Readers.

1 3 5 7 9 10 8 6 4 2

LIBRARY OF CONGRESS CATALOGING-IN-PUBLICATION DATA
McDonnell, Christine.
Ballet bug / by Christine McDonnell ; illustrated by Martha Doty.
p. cm.
Summary: When Bea becomes interested in ballet, she starts taking classes,
auditions for The Nutcracker, and makes a new best friend, but
also must cope with some nasty classmates and a possible conflict
between playing hockey and dancing.
ISBN 0-670-03508-4 (hardcover)
[1. Ballet dancing—Fiction. 2. Nutcracker (Choreographic work)—
Fiction. 3. Hockey—Fiction.] I. Doty, Martha, ill. II. Title.
PZ7.M47843 Bal 2001
[Fic]—dc21
2001002317

Printed in U.S.A.
Set in Fairfield
Designed by Kelley McIntyre

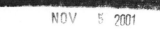

*F*or Terry, with fond memories of
cold rinks, hot coffee, hockey pads,
and ballet shoes

TABLE OF CONTENTS

Ballet Bug

CHAPTER 1

$\mathcal{B}$UG $\mathcal{B}$ITE

Bea Nash: her name was printed on the pink envelope. The card inside showed a ballerina balanced on one foot on top of a white cake. Ribbons from a pair of ballet shoes formed the words *A Ballerina's Birthday—Come join the dance.*

Bea knew the card must be from Rebecca. Rebecca was crazy about ballet. Her school binder and her pencil case both had ballerinas on the front. She even had an eraser shaped like a ballet shoe.

Bea showed the card to her mother. Mrs. Nash checked the date. "You have hockey practice until seven. I'm sure Rebecca won't mind if you get there a little late. Or you could skip practice."

"Skip hockey? Never!" Bea said. She read the card again. *It's a sleep over. We'll dance all night.* "Dance all night?"

"It's just an expression, honey. It means you'll have lots of fun."

"There better be games," Bea grumbled. "I'm not dancing."

Mrs. Nash was already making plans. "We can stop on the way to the hockey rink and pick out a present."

Friday afternoon, Bea strapped hockey pads onto her legs and shoulders and pulled on long socks, padded shorts, and her team jersey. Glimpsing herself in the mirror she chuckled. With her hockey pads on, she looked like a reflection in a fun-house mirror. She packed jeans and pajamas in a duffel bag and added her toothbrush and Amos, the stuffed dog she still tucked under her arm at night. She lugged the duffel, a sleeping bag, and her hockey stick out to the car.

At Toys for All, Bea wandered up and down the aisles. "*Everyone* will give her ballet stuff. I want something different," she said.

Mrs. Nash made suggestions: a puzzle? an art kit? a board game? a stuffed animal? Every time Bea shook her head. "Ten more minutes," Mrs. Nash said. "Choose something while I grab some wrapping paper."

Finally Bea found a red bubble-gum bank filled with shiny gum balls. "I bet it's the only present that has nothing to do with ballet."

"I'll wrap it while you're skating," Mrs. Nash said.

Practice was hard! Coach made the team do speed drills until Bea was panting and sweat dripped off her chin. During scrimmage she scored two goals.

"Almost a hat trick," she boasted to her mother when practice ended.

"Like the Mexican dance?"

"Mom! A hat trick is when you score three goals in one game. Fans throw their hats on the ice."

"Imagine that," said Mrs. Nash. "I guess I'll have to bring a hat."

"I feel like a sponge," Bea said. "I need a shower."

"You can take one at Rebecca's," her mother said.

"Won't that be rude?" Bea asked. "Hi, I'm here for the party. Where's your shower?"

"You have to change out of your hockey things anyway," Mrs. Nash pointed out. "I'll explain."

Rebecca's mother led Bea to the upstairs bathroom and left her a thick towel to dry off with. Bea waited until the shower was steamy before stepping in. She tipped her face up into the stream of hot water, then let the spray drum against her back and shoulders. After a hard practice, the hot shower felt so good she would have stayed in until her fingers puckered, but she didn't want to miss the party.

Bea came downstairs just as the pizza deliveryman rang the doorbell. She joined the others at the dining room table, feeling self-conscious about her wet hair. But no one seemed to notice. Rebecca waved from the head of the table. She wore a pink sweatshirt with ballet slippers on it. Her hair was pulled back by ballerina barrettes.

All the gifts piled on the side table were wrapped in pink or silver paper, or paper with ballerinas and ballet shoes. All except Bea's—her wrapping paper had red and blue comic-book characters yelling, "Happy Birthday!" Maybe I should have picked out a ballet-type present, she worried.

Hockey practice always made Bea hungry. She ate three slices of pizza. Next, Rebecca opened her presents. The first three presents were a music box, a puzzle, and a charm bracelet: ballerinas on all three. When Rebecca picked up Bea's gift, she laughed at the wrapping paper. Then she opened the box and squealed, "I always wanted one of these! Thanks, Bea!"

Bea settled back to enjoy the cake and ice cream. After the guests were stuffed, the games began. The girls played Twister, slipping, sliding, and laughing as they moved their hands and feet. Next, sitting in a circle, they played Murder. Then it was time for Sardines.

"Are any rooms off limits?" Rebecca asked her mother.

"Just the kitchen and my closet," her mother said.

The first hiding place was behind the drapes in the dining room. Bea found the sardines easily because the drapes looked lumpy. The shower stall was the next spot. They squeezed behind the frosted glass. But someone began to giggle and gave them away. When they hid in the basement, behind the furnace, it made Bea think of spiders. The game ended with all twelve girls stuffed under Rebecca's parents' bed, trying not to sneeze.

"Movie time," Rebecca's mother called. "Everyone change into pajamas."

The girls spread their sleeping bags over the den rug and sat cross-legged or sprawled on top. Rebecca's mother carried in soda and popcorn. "Everybody comfy?" she asked. Rebecca started the VCR.

It was a dance movie, of course. Bea sighed. Dance, dance, dance. Why does everything have to be about ballet? After a few minutes Bea realized it was the story of Cinderella, her very favorite fairy tale. The dancer in the leading role was almost as small as a child. She could bend effortlessly and leap as if there was no gravity on the stage. She could also spin, glide, float, and lift her leg high above her head as if it was as easy as just walking.

Dancing made the story fresh. The music captured Cinderella's sadness and loneliness. Then the ugly stepsisters, played by two male dancers, cheered things up with clumsy steps and clowning. They wore padded bosoms and frilly dresses. One sister was tall and skinny, with a frizzy red wig. The other was stuffed like a couch, with a black wart on her chin. What a contrast to Cinderella, slender and plain in a peasant dress and apron.

As the movie continued, some of the girls talked and played cards, but Bea sat with her chin on her hands

watching every step. After Cinderella's wedding, Bea lay back on her sleeping bag and closed her eyes, trying to remember the music and the steps. I wish I could move like that, she thought.

The rest of the weekend Bea was busy with a hockey game on Saturday afternoon and a visit to her grandparents' house on Sunday. Every so often an image from *Cinderella* came to her mind: Cinderella alone on stage holding her mother's locket and pretending to dance with her; the stepsisters shoving each other aside to preen in front of a tall mirror; dancers twirling at the palace ball.

Sunday night, before going up for bed, Bea found her mother in the living room, working on the Sunday crossword puzzle. Bigfoot, the family's fat, gray cat, lay across the back of her chair.

"He looks like your fur collar," Bea said.

Mrs. Nash reached back and scratched the cat's head. "He likes the warm lamp. What's up, Bumblebee?"

Bea described *Cinderella.* "The dancers moved even faster than skaters. And could they ever jump! Do you think it's too late to start ballet?"

"I never thought I'd hear you ask for ballet lessons," Mrs. Nash said, shaking her head in wonder. "What about hockey?"

"I want to do both," Bea said.

"Are you sure you can handle it?"

Bea nodded.

Mrs. Nash thought for a minute, tapping her pencil

against her teeth. Bea waited. Finally her mother said, "I'll see what I can do. Sounds to me like you've been bitten by the ballet bug."

"Thanks, Mom," Bea said, giving her mother an extra big hug.

"Sleep tight. Don't let the bedbugs bite," her mother said, giving Bea a good-night kiss.

"Ballet bug," Bea corrected. "Too late. It already got me!"

CHAPTER 2

GETTING STARTED

Bea waited with her mother at the counter of Dancing Delights. "You're sure you want to do this?" Mrs. Nash asked, one more time.

"Positive!" Bea bounced on her toes.

The saleswoman showed them to a bench and measured Bea's foot. Then she disappeared behind a curtain and returned with two boxes of shoes and two navy leotards. She fit the shoes first. "They should be snug," she explained.

Then she handed Bea a leotard and pointed to a dressing room. When Bea pulled on the leotard, her underwear bunched up underneath. She looked like a lumpy laundry bag.

"Mom!" she groaned. "I'm all wrinkly!"

Mrs. Nash peeked around the curtain and laughed. "You do look like a sack of potatoes. Don't worry. That's just your underwear. The leotard will be smooth when you wear tights underneath." Mrs. Nash tugged the leotard's leg elastic and pulled at the neckline. "This fits. Get dressed and we'll have them wrap it all up."

As they waited at the counter, Bea watched an older girl model a rose-colored leotard.

"Why can't I wear a color like that?" Bea asked.

"Every class has a different color," her mother said. "That deep pink must be a more advanced class."

The saleswoman showed Mrs. Nash where to sew the elastic across the front of the ballet shoes. She packed the shoebox, leotards, and two pairs of pink tights into a silver bag and handed it to Bea. "Work hard," she said. Bea wondered why she didn't say, "Have fun." "Work hard" sounded more like school then dancing.

Monday afternoon, the first day of ballet class, Bea followed a stream of girls into the dressing room. She found a hook for her coat and stuffed her sneakers into a cubby. Girls were tugging sweaters over their heads, pulling on tights and leotards. Two girls at the mirror twisted their hair into buns and skewered them with hairpins. Talk and laughter filled the air. Everyone seemed to know someone else.

Everyone except me, Bea thought. I wish Rebecca was here. Why does her class have to meet on different days?

"Hi, Bea!" said a friendly voice behind her. Bea turned to find Margaret, a girl she knew from summer camp, pulling a leotard out of her backpack. "I didn't know you took ballet," Margaret said.

"This is my first day," Bea said. She tugged at the neck of her leotard. "It feels so strange."

"What class are you in?"

Bea told her and Margaret offered to show her the way. "I'm right across the hall."

Margaret pointed out Studio C. "That's your room. Good luck. Madame's a very good teacher."

Bea's footsteps echoed as she crossed the empty room. She shivered and wrapped her arms around her waist. The door opened and a large lady headed toward the piano and began to arrange her music on the piano stand. She smiled at Bea and began to play. Bea leaned against the barre and listened.

Next a woman dressed all in black with silver hair pulled in a bun swept in with her head held up high. A group of noisy girls followed her. "Oh Madame, please . . . No, it's my turn, Madame . . . But I should go first this time, Madame. . . ."

"Sssh, sssh, *mes enfants*," the woman said with a sweep of her arm. "Take your places at the barre for warm-up."

Bea found space at the end of the line. She followed the moves of the other girls as best she could. Soon the teacher drifted toward her. "What have we here? You are new." This wasn't a question. "You have never studied bal-

let. Never mind, my pet. Madame will show you."

She rearranged Bea's feet and hands. She placed her fingers gently under Bea's chin and tapped it up. Then last, she put her hands on either side of Bea's waist. "Belly in, *derrière* down," she instructed. "Tuck, tuck, tuck." With each "tuck," Madame patted Bea's bottom. "What is your name?"

"Bea Nash."

"Bea-ah-treesse." Madame pronounced it in three syllables, with an *s* sound at the end like a snake's hiss. "Bea-u-ti-ful name, Bea-ah-treesse. Beautiful name for ballet."

Madame returned to the front of the room and continued the lesson. First position, second position, five in all. Arms and hands just so. *Plié. Jeté. Demi plié.* "*One* two three four, *one* two three four," Madame counted as she demonstrated a series of steps in time to the music. Two by two, moving across the room from one corner to the other, the girls practiced the combination.

The pianist played music with four counts: *one* two three four, emphasized. Bea could hear the beat, but some pairs of girls were way off tempo and Madame made them go back and start over. "No no no no *no!* Listen, you must listen to the music."

Madame gave the signal nod. *One* two three four, *one* two three four, Bea counted in her head. She tried to make her feet move to the music. She didn't have time to think about being graceful. She focused on her feet and

13

the count. By the time she reached the corner she was breathless. Madame nodded, and Bea thought she might have smiled.

They practiced the steps many times. Bea could tell which dancers thought they were best. A pair of twins with blond braids giggled and rolled their eyes as the other students moved across the floor. They whispered behind their hands to each other and then laughed in a mean way. But Bea noticed that they weren't the best dancers. They did the steps but their movements were stiff. They reminded Bea of windup toys. Whenever another dancer earned Madame's praise, the twins pouted and tried to trip or bump her as she passed. They left Bea alone. That's because I'm not good enough, Bea thought. Not yet.

At the end of the class, Madame called one twin up front to demonstrate a curtsy. "Erin, come and show our new student how we end the class."

Happy to be singled out, the twin exaggerated every movement. Her neck arched stiffly and when she dipped toward the floor, she pushed her bottom up like a cat stretching.

"Oh no no no no," Madame stuttered, moving quickly toward her with hands outstretched to correct the posture. "Every line must be soft and long. Why push up the *derrière*? You must pay attention to the movements, to the line." She sent her back and called another dancer up to show the curtsy.

Erin stepped back in the line and glared at Madame.

After the demonstration, the whole class curtsied and said, "Thank you, Madame." All except Erin, who flounced out of the room.

Margaret was waiting for Bea in the changing room. "How did it go?" she asked. Bea made a sad clown face.

"Don't worry," Margaret said. "It's just your first day. You'll pick it up. But you love it don't you?"

Bea nodded but she wasn't sure if she loved it yet. It was harder than she'd expected. She certainly wasn't gliding and leaping. But at least she wasn't stumbling either. You didn't learn to skate in one day, she told herself.

"It's hard to make my feet do the steps," she said.

"It gets easier," Margaret said.

Bea finished changing and waved good-bye to Margaret. "See you Wednesday," she said.

Her mother was waiting outside. She handed Bea a juice box when she'd climbed in and buckled her seat belt. "Have fun?" Mrs. Nash asked.

"It was hard!" Bea said. "A girl I know from camp showed me around. She's in a higher level class but I see her when we're changing. I think we'll be friends."

CHAPTER 3

No Hockey?

Bea had ballet on Monday and Wednesday. Margaret's class met on those days, plus Friday as well. "Lucky I'm not in your class," Bea told Margaret. "I've got hockey practice on Friday."

"Ice hockey? I thought that was for boys," Margaret said.

"Not anymore," Bea said. "There are plenty of girls' teams now."

"Don't you worry about getting hurt?" Margaret wiggled into her tights. "I thought hockey had lots of pushing and knocking down."

"Not in girls' hockey. We don't check. That's what it's

16

called when you block somebody with your body and push them or hold them against the boards."

"Boards? I thought you were on ice."

Bea laughed. "The boards are the sides of the rink."

Margaret laughed, too. "You mean what I always hang on to when I go skating." She demonstrated. One step forward, wobble, cling to the side. "I'm a terrible skater."

"You're just scared. Skate with me, and once you see how easy it is, you'll let go of the boards. I'll show you," Bea offered.

"Would you really? It looks like so much fun, gliding along, just like dancing," Margaret said.

"I don't glide in ballet yet," Bea said.

"It's only your second week," Margaret said. "You'll glide."

"So will you, on ice," Bea promised. "As soon as the town rink opens, we'll go together."

Margaret nodded and linked arms with Bea. "Can't be late for Madame," she said, speeding up her steps. "You don't ever want to be late for Madame."

Madame smiled at Bea when she came in. "Ah, Bea-ah-treesse. I see you are friends with Mar-gar-eet. Such a bea-u-ti-ful dancer."

As Bea stepped up to the barre for the warmup, the closest twin scowled at her. Bea was glad when another student took the spot beside her, shielding her from the twin's glare.

Class ended ten minutes early. "Come and sit, *mes*

chéries," Madame said. "Turn yourselves into a circle." She waved her hand in an arc. The class sat cross-legged on the floor. Madame handed a sheaf of blue paper to the student on her right. "Pass these, please," she said. "Many of you are new to the school. We must review the rules."

The twins made smug faces.

Rules? What kind of rules could there be in ballet? Bea wondered. There's no offsides in dance. You can't foul. Nobody trips anyone. Maybe there's a no-kicking rule. She imagined a ballerina aiming her toe at her partner's chin.

Madame waited until the papers were passed around the circle. Meanwhile, Bea read the list. Some of the rules she had already figured out: be on time; no talking in class; leotards and ballet slippers must be worn; hair should be off the neck and face. Other rules were just like school: no running; no chewing gum. But the last item on the list surprised her. "Participation in competitive sports is strongly discouraged."

What does "strongly discouraged" mean? Are they saying I can't play sports? Bea wondered.

Madame perched her glasses on the end of her nose so she could peer over them at the class. She began to read the rules, stopping after each one to peer out with eyebrows raised. "Do you understand why this is important, *mes chéries?* This rule is for your safety." When she reached the last line, she read it slowly, then took her glasses off and used them to gesture with.

"This is not a rule. It is a suggestion. We are only a

school for the ballet. We cannot control what you do outside of this building. But we will make suggestions that are helpful for you as you continue to study ballet. For instance, I tell you to eat fruit and vegetables, not candy and soda. A dancer must be light and quick. If you start now, you will form a taste for the foods that make you strong and light, not slow and heavy. That is one recommendation."

Madame waved her glasses like a wand. "I know you will agree, yes?" The class nodded as if hypnotized.

Madame continued. "What is the purpose of all this training, all your practice and hard work in learning the steps and the way the body is held in ballet? What sense is there to learn all that and then to go out onto the gymnasium, onto the athletic field to injure yourselves? Perhaps you will hurt your leg, your arm. How can your feet move with precision here in the dance studio if outside, in sports, you go clump clump clump?" She stomped on the floor, accenting each *clump*.

The class giggled. Most nodded in agreement. But not Bea. I don't go clump clump clump in hockey, Bea thought. Hockey is just as precise as ballet. It matters where you stand, how far you lean, what angle you shoot from. Everything matters. That's what the coach always says.

Madame went on to discuss sleep, but Bea was only half listening. I'll never give up hockey, she thought. Do they expect us to give up gym? Gym's competitive. There's basketball, flag football, floor hockey. Bea shook her head.

Gym was her favorite part of school.

"Bea-ah-treesse, why are you shaking your head back and forth like a pony? You don't agree that we need sleep to fuel our bodies?" Madame narrowed her eyes like a hawk staring at its victim.

Bea wiggled. "No, Madame, I mean yes. Of course we need sleep." She felt a blush rising up her neck.

Madame shook her head in disappointment. "Girls, girls, girls. I am talking about your health. Bea-ah-treesse, don't tell me that you plan to eat potato chips and doughnuts or to play sports like a hooligan. I am certain that is not the case. Try to pay attention, *ma chérie*."

"Yes, Madame," Bea croaked, her voice caught in her throat in embarrassment. "Sorry, Madame."

When class was dismissed, after the final curtsy, Bea hurried to get changed. Margaret was already gone. The twins had spread their clothes all over the bench nearest to Bea's cubby.

"Tsk, tsk, Bea-ah-treesse, you must pay attention," one twin mocked. "Bad, bad Bea-ah-treesse. Madame doesn't like it when you don't listen."

"Be careful, Bea-ah-treesse." The other twin smirked. "You don't want to make Madame angry."

Bea quickly pulled her jeans up over her tights and leotard. The twins were like mosquitoes whining near her ear. What they needed was a slap. Bea left without saying good-bye.

Later, at home, she fished the crumpled list out of her

ballet bag and brought it into the kitchen. Mrs. Nash was rubbing a chicken with olive oil and garlic. She slapped the bird on its chest. "I'm giving you a good massage, aren't I, Chicky?"

"Mom, you're talking to a dead chicken!" Bea pointed out.

Mrs. Nash shrugged. "I talk to the cat, too."

"Bigfoot's alive, Mom. The chicken is dead."

"I hope so. Would you eat a live chicken?"

Bea groaned. Sometimes her mother was too silly. "They gave out rules in ballet class. Some are strange."

Mrs. Nash washed the oil off her hands, dried them, and took the blue sheet that Bea offered.

"Read the last line, Mom. Does that mean I can't play hockey?"

"*Strongly discouraged* is about as close to no as you can get without saying the word. They'd rather you didn't play, Bumblebee, but they can't force you. It's your choice."

Bea punched the air in victory. "Thanks, Mom." She hugged her mother around her waist. "I can play, I can play," she chanted as she left the room.

CHAPTER 4

*H*OCKEY *AND* *B*ALLET

Bea didn't talk about her ice hockey practices or her games at ballet. She didn't trust the twins. Who knows when they might be eavesdropping, she figured. She and Margaret talked mostly about dancing. They traded ballet books, ballet videos, and music. Margaret described ballets she'd seen. Bea told her about *Cinderella*.

At hockey practice, Bea didn't mention ballet. No one else on the team took dance classes. What could be more different than hockey and ballet? At ballet class she wore a skinny leotard and flimsy ballet slippers. For hockey, she strapped on bulky pads that made her waddle until she got on the ice. Ballet and hockey were two parts of her life that didn't connect, Bea figured. But then, one Friday practice, they did connect.

"We have a guest teacher today," the coach announced when the team came out on the ice. "He's here to help speed up our footwork. So give him all you've got."

The guest was a wiry man with a scar below his left eye. Bea wondered if he'd been hit by a hockey puck. "Call me Burt," he said to the team. "We're going to do some fancy footwork together. Don't be afraid to ask questions. If it gets confusing, stop me and I'll show you again. You won't be needing sticks today."

The team skated to the side of the rink and stacked their sticks against the bench.

"Okay, girls, line up across the blue line here and keep your eyes on my skates. Here's the first combination."

Burt gave a little hop and then stepped left over right, right over left, left twice, right twice. He repeated the pattern until he reached the far goal. Then he glided back in long loops.

"Got it?" he asked. When no one answered, he repeated the steps slowly. "Your turn," he said. "Follow me. One, two, three, go." He led the line forward, calling out each step.

Bea was near the center, skating right behind Burt. By the second repetition, she caught the rhythm of the drill. It played in her mind as a tune: da, da, da-de-dah, da-de-dah. The steps came easily to her. When she reached the goal cage, the rest of the team was still floundering as they tried to cross their feet. They looked more like seasick sailors than skaters.

"Not bad," Burt said. "Let's try another. Line up in front of the goal. Watch my feet." He did a new combination with three steps to the right, a glide to the left, and then the reverse, three steps left, glide right. Right away a new tune floated into Bea's head: de-de-de-dum, de-de-de-dum. She danced the length of the rink. Burt rewarded her with a wink.

"Footwork, ladies, is the key to a good offense," Burt said. "If you can side step, switch direction, change speed, turn, and reverse, you can get by anyone."

He taught them one combination after another, some simple, some fancy. Even the coach had trouble following the last series of steps. But not Bea. For every new set of steps, she made up a tune. It always helped. In her head she was dancing while her feet were skating.

At the end of practice, Burt patted her head as she passed by on her way to the bench. "Keep practicing, kid. Soon you'll outskate the pros."

Coach plopped down beside Bea with a huff and a groan. "What a workout!" he said, wiping his forehead on the sleeve of his jersey. "What's your secret, Nash? Where did you learn to do fancy footwork?"

Bea shrugged and grinned. "It was fun," she said.

"Fun?" Coach groaned. "It was tough! How do you keep the steps straight?"

Bea shrugged again. Ballet, she thought. But she didn't say it out loud.

CHAPTER 5

BAD HAIR DAY

The telephone rang on Monday night, right after the family had finished eating dinner. Mrs. Nash stayed on the phone for a long time. Bea cleared the table and loaded the dishwasher. She was arguing with her brother Andy over who should wipe the table and counters when her mother returned.

"Please, no squabbling. Not tonight," Mrs. Nash said. "That was Grandma Jean on the phone. Great-Granny Pat is very sick. I'm driving up and I'll probably be away for the rest of the week. Daddy will be here looking after things but he's going to need a lot of help."

"What's wrong with Great-Granny Pat?" Andy asked.

26

Bea held her breath waiting for the answer. Great-Granny Pat was so old that Bea couldn't even guess her age. When Bea hugged her, she felt tiny and frail, a little bird woman.

"They aren't sure yet," Mrs. Nash said, smoothing Andy's hair out of his eyes. "She fell getting out of bed. The doctors think she may have had a stroke. You know how very old she is. Grandma Jean is so worried."

Bea's father gave her mother a big hug. Bea and Andy joined in and circled her with their arms. When the hug ended, Bea saw tears on her mother's cheeks.

"Don't worry, Mom," Bea said.

"Thanks, sweetie. Great-Granny Pat is such a funny old lady. You two are lucky to have had a chance to know her." Mrs. Nash wiped her eyes.

"When are you leaving?" Mr. Nash asked.

"As soon as I throw some clothes in a bag."

"I'll make you a thermos of coffee for the road," he said. "We don't want you to drift off while you're driving."

While Mrs. Nash packed, Bea and Andy made get-well cards. Andy drew an elephant.

"An elephant on a get-well card?" Bea said.

"I made the knees all wrinkly," Andy said. "Elephants live a long time. That should cheer up Great-Granny Pat."

Bea drew a hand holding a big bunch of flowers and glued it to a folded paper spring. When the card opened, the flowers popped out and jiggled.

Mrs. Nash kissed both children good-bye. "Be good.

Don't fight. Help your father." Her words drifted back over her shoulder as she headed toward the car.

Tuesday morning Mr. Nash made pancakes as a treat. He even gave Bea and Andy a lift to school on his way to the office.

"Come right home after school," he said. "Bea, you're in charge. Whatever she says goes, okay Andy? I'll be home early."

Bea did exactly as her father had asked although she would rather have stayed in the park and played touch football with her friends.

On Wednesday, Andy went home with a friend after school so Mr. Nash could drive Bea to her ballet class. The house was empty when Bea got home. She made a snack, apple slices with peanut butter, and carried the plate upstairs. Bigfoot padded in front of her, leading the way to her bedroom. The big gray cat jumped up on Bea's bed, circled twice and settled in on top of the quilt. He watched Bea with his green eyes half shut.

Bea pulled open her top drawer and rummaged for her leotard and tights. She couldn't find any. She ran downstairs and checked the clean clothes pile. Oh no, the laundry never got done, she thought. Back upstairs, she dumped her drawers upside down on the floor and pawed frantically through the mound of underwear, pajamas, and T-shirts. No sign of a navy leotard or pink tights.

The front door opened and closed and her father called, "Hi, Bea! Ready for ballet?"

Panic made Bea's voice too small to be heard. Mr. Nash came upstairs looking for her. "What's wrong?" he said. "Did something happen at school?"

Bea shook her head. "Ballet," she squeaked. "I can't go." She sucked in a breath of air. "I don't have a leotard." Then she hiccuped.

Her father was confused. "No leotard?"

"They're dirty! Both leotards! Mom forgot to do the wash," Bea wailed.

"Mom didn't have time to do the laundry before she left," Mr. Nash said. "I'm the one who forgot. Come on. Let's find them."

Together they sifted through the hamper in Bea's room. "Here's one," Bea said, holding up a crumpled navy leotard.

Mr. Nash fished another wad of navy blue cloth from the bathroom hamper. "Let's see which one is cleaner," he said.

"Dad! I can't wear a dirty leotard," Bea said.

"It's just for one class. Who's going to know?" her father said.

"I'll smell."

"So? Fish smell. Horses smell. Bigfoot here smells, don't you old guy?" Mr. Nash said, winking at Bea. He sniffed both leotards. "This one is a little ripe," he admitted. "Must have been at the bottom of the heap. But this one will do. Here. Check it."

Bea wrinkled her nose. She held the leotard between

29

two fingers as if it had cooties. Sniff sniff. It wasn't bad.

"But what about tights?" Bea asked.

"What's wrong with the ones you wear to church?" her father asked. He fished a pair of white tights out of the mound of clothes on the floor.

"Those aren't the right kind," Bea said. Her voice started to quiver again. "Dance tights are thicker. Besides, they've got to be pink."

"Sweetheart, these will do for today. I can explain to your teacher. It's an emergency situation here, right?"

Bea nodded glumly.

"Change fast and we'll go." Her father rubbed the wrinkles between his eyebrows.

Bea pulled on the tights and the not-quite-clean leotard, covered them with a big sweatshirt and stepped into her clogs.

"My hair!" She stopped in the middle of the hall. "Who's going to do my hair?"

Her father would have to do it. There wasn't anyone else. She carried the basket with all her hairpins and nets downstairs and set it on the kitchen table. "You've got to fix my hair," she told her father.

"It looks fine," Mr. Nash said.

Bea shook her head. "It's got to go up." She pointed to the top of her head.

Mr. Nash shook his head. "That's out of my league, sweetie. I can't even get my own hair to go up." He pointed to the bald spot on top of his head.

30

"Don't kid, Dad. It's a rule. Hair's got to be up off the neck. I'll tell you what to do, okay?"

"I'll try," he promised.

"First I make a ponytail," Bea said. She pulled her hair back and wound an elastic around twice. "Now you twist it in a circle and pin it."

Bea held the hairpins while her father struggled. She could hear him sigh.

"Your hair keeps sliding out," he complained.

"Mom just twists it and pins it. That's all," Bea said.

"She must have some special trick to make it stay in place. Maybe she nails it to your scalp. How about glue? Or nails?" he teased.

"Dad!" Bea yelped.

"I'm desperate. You'll miss class if we don't get this done fast. Don't we have some sort of hair goo?"

Bea shook her head.

"How about Vaseline? That's sticky," her father said. "Run upstairs and get the jar."

Armed with the Vaseline, Mr. Nash made a bun.

"Now wrap a net around it and stick in some more hairpins." Bea handed the hairnet over her shoulder. Mr. Nash fumbled some more trying to untangle the hairnet. He finally managed to slip it around Bea's crooked bun.

Bea made it to class on time, thanks to a shortcut her father knew. She raced through the studio door just as Madame was saying, "*Ah-ten-see-on, mes chéries.*" Slipping into a space along the barre, she took a deep breath.

For the first set of warmups the class faced the windows. Bea held the barre in her left hand and followed Madame's instructions. She brushed her foot forward and back, pointing first in front and then behind. Point, flex, brush, point, flex, brush. Next she bent to each side, then forward.

For the next set of exercises, the class faced the mirror and placed both hands on the barre. Bea gawked at her reflection. What a mess! Her leotard was wrinkled. Her tights stood out from the row of pink tights on either side of her. And her hair! It was greasy with Vaseline. Her bun was slipping toward her ear. Bea tried to keep her head still and hoped the bun wouldn't slide off. Up on the toes and down. Feet parallel then opened out in a V. Up, down, up, down. Knee bends next with feet opened out.

Madame came along the line adjusting shoulders and checking ankles as each girl rose on her toes. When she reached Bea, she paused and touched the back of her head where the gooey Vaseline coated the bun. She raised her eyebrows in a silent question.

"My great-granny's sick, so my mom's away," Bea whispered. "My dad's in charge this week."

Madame nodded. She adjusted Bea's bun and pinned it in the middle of her head. With a grimace, she wiped her fingers together to rub off the goo. "I hope your great-grandmama is better soon," she whispered in Bea's ear. "Next time, if your mother is still away, I will put your hair up for you. Come to class a few minutes early. Tell your papa not to bother with this." Madame gave Bea's shoulder a little squeeze before moving to the next girl.

After class, as Bea was changing, the twins, Erin and Caitlin, paused by her bench. "Greaser," Erin said. "Why didn't you try glue?"

"I thought of it," Bea muttered.

"I saw Madame yelling at you," Caitlin gloated. "You don't even have on the right tights. You look like a bum."

"A ballet bum," Erin added.

Bea finished tying her sneakers. She pulled on her jacket and slung her ballet bag over her shoulder. "See you next week," she said. It was easy to ignore the twins with Madame's kind words in her mind.

Mrs. Nash came home on Sunday. Great-Granny Pat was feeling better. Bea went to ballet on Monday in a clean leotard and pink tights. Her bun was smack on the top of her head, right in the center. The twins couldn't call her a ballet bum this time.

Bea told Madame that her great-grandmother was better now.

"I am happy to hear it," Madame said. "Remember, Bea-ah-treesse, next time there is a problem, come to me."

CHAPTER 6
$\mathcal{N}$UTCRACKER $\mathcal{T}$RYOUTS

Bea sat on the living room carpet watching Saturday morning cartoons. She stretched her legs open wide in a V and leaned toward the floor, trying to inch her legs further apart. Some girls in ballet class could stretch their legs into a perfect split, lean forward, and rest their chins in the palm of their hands, as comfortable as cats.

The bell rang and Bea pried her legs loose and answered the door. Pete, her best friend and next-door neighbor, stood on the top step wearing his roller blades. "Hockey time!" He pointed toward the end of the block where nets were set up. A few skaters were already weaving and taking shots.

"I can't. It's tryout day for *The Nutcracker*," Bea said. "If I get a part I'll be onstage with real ballerinas."

Pete wasn't impressed. "Ohhh man, I told the guys you'd play. Is Andy around?"

"He's probably up in his room playing with his action figures."

Pete clumped up the stairs in his roller blades and came down followed by Bea's younger brother. Bea helped Andy strap on knee and elbow pads and held the door open for him. He wobbled down the steps and skated after Pete, waving his stick wildly in the air to keep his balance. Bea wished she was skating, too. A fall morning like this, with the trees bright and the air crisp, was perfect for street hockey. Too bad tryouts had to be on Saturday.

"Better get changed, sweetie," her mother said. "Not a good idea to wear pajamas to the tryouts." She ruffled Bea's hair and turned off the TV.

Bea did a pirouette with her pajama pants flapping. "Do you think I'll get a part?"

"My crystal ball says maybe. Go change while I pack some snacks. This may take all day."

Bea thought her mother was joking until she pushed open the front door at the ballet school and found the hall jammed with parents and children. Mrs. Nash wormed her way to the front desk. Bea tried to follow but got stuck, crunched by little girls with buns and ladies waving pink registration papers. Finally her mother reappeared holding a square with number 118. "Don't let go of my hand," she shouted and pulled Bea through the throng. "Your age group is upstairs."

They elbowed a path through the crowd. "What a mob! It's worse than the subway at rush hour," Mrs. Nash said. "There are a lot of crazy parents here. No wonder they call them nutmoms."

"Why?" Bea asked.

Her mother pinned the number to the front of her leotard. "Nut for Nutcracker and also because some parents are nutty about their child's part. They want a big role for their little girls." She held Bea's shoulders and gave her a stern look. "Bea, if this stops being fun, you'll tell me, won't you, sweetie? Promise?"

The large practice hall stretched the whole length of the building, with windows as high as the ceiling and mirrors with barres in front. A woman at the door wrote Bea's name and her number on a list. "Line up along the wall facing the windows. Parents wait outside, please."

Mrs. Nash took Bea's bag and jacket and gave her a kiss on the forehead. "Good luck, Bumblebee."

Bea turned toward the other girls, who were leaning on the barre, stretching, sitting on the floor, or dancing nervous jigs. They formed a striped ribbon of different colored leotards: pink, purple, red, blue. More girls came through the door, numbers fluttering on their chests. The ribbon grew longer.

The twins, Erin and Caitlin, strutted in together. Bea started to wave but stopped. At class, they either snubbed

her or teased her. They certainly wouldn't make her feel more at ease today. A few others from class joined the line, their navy leotards dull against the bright colors of girls from other schools. Finally Rebecca arrived. She waved happily at Bea and skipped across the room. "Aren't you excited?" she squealed.

Then Margaret raced in, ballet bag banging against her hip. "Am I late? The bus didn't come for ages."

The woman at the door smiled. "We're just about to start. Catch your breath, change your shoes, and line up."

Margaret pulled off her jacket, sneakers, jeans, and sweater, and slipped on her ballet shoes. Bea moved over to make a space for her, and Margaret thanked her with a grin. "Nervous? I always am," she whispered. She squeezed Bea's arm.

"What do they make us do?" Bea asked.

"They teach a combination, and we dance across the room," Margaret said.

"With everyone watching?" Bea was horrified. There were at least a hundred girls plus tons of grown-ups.

"It's not hard," Rebecca said. "Everybody does the same thing."

"With so many kids trying out, they'll have us go in groups," Margaret said.

Bea cringed. At camp swim meets, five girls raced at a time. She had been last in her heat every week, swallowing froth from all the kicking feet. At least she wouldn't get water up her nose today!

A young woman in a black leotard and skirt walked to the middle of the room and clapped her hands twice. "All right, girls and boys, let's get started."

Bea hadn't noticed the boys in the group. They stood in a clump, wearing white T-shirts, black tights, and black ballet slippers. They didn't even look uncomfortable, outnumbered and surrounded by girls.

The woman divided them into four groups. Bea, Margaret, and Rebecca were together in the first batch. The twins were in the second batch.

"Watch carefully," the woman in black said. "I'll demonstrate three times. Each group will do the steps together, and then two by two." She nodded to the pianist. It was a very simple dance and the music was easy to follow. Margaret danced the steps along with the teacher by the second round. Bea copied her. This wouldn't be so bad if only there weren't so many people here, she thought.

"Ignore the others," Margaret whispered, reading Bea's mind. "Make your eyes blurry and listen to the music. And smile!"

"Group one, form two lines," the lady directed. This resulted in a snarl of leotards. "Stop where you are," the lady shrilled. She swooped down and sorted them into rows that stretched from wall to wall. Margaret and Bea were directly behind Rebecca.

The piano began and the teacher called, "One, two, three, begin!" The first line danced across the floor. Some children were ahead of the music and some lagged behind. A few mixed up the steps, going right instead of left, bumping into their neighbors. The lady in black shook her head in dismay. "Next line," she called. "Listen for the beat in the music, children. One, two, three, begin."

Bea counted in her head and let the music guide her. She forgot about the other dancers. Holding her head up and pasting a smile on, she repeated the combination of steps again and again until she reached the windows.

"Again," the woman commanded. The lines reassembled and started over. Bea began to enjoy herself. It was a skipping little dance, and she gave some bounce to the steps this time.

"And now by twos," the woman said.

The children made one long snake line and, two by two, danced across the room from corner to corner. Margaret was ahead of Bea. She gave the steps flair, connecting them into a springy dance.

Bea listened to the music and waited for the nod to begin. She tried to stay even with her partner while keeping her steps light and happy. She reached the far corner and then scurried back to the line again. Margaret linked arms with her. "That was perfect, right on the beat."

They danced across in pairs once more while the adults wrote notes on the clipboards. Next, the second group lined up. When it was time to dance two by two, the twins were paired with other children. They both wore snooty looks. But their steps were off beat and they couldn't stay even with their partners.

Finally, after all four groups had danced, the lady in black announced, "Parts will be ready at three o'clock in the lobby downstairs."

Bea and Rebecca waited for Margaret to gather her pile of clothes. "My mom's waiting. How about you?" Bea said.

"I came by myself," Margaret said. "This is my mom's weekend shift. She's a nurse."

Bea's mother was standing by the stairs with Rebecca's mother. Mrs. Nash invited Margaret to join them for lunch. "We all need some fresh air. If I have to spend another minute with these nutmoms, I'll go nuts!"

Wind scuttled leaves along the sidewalk, and overhead clouds inched across the sky like a herd of sheep. The girls ran from lamppost to lamppost, twirling around each one while the mothers searched for a promising lunch place.

"Look at this! A luncheonette with a counter. I haven't seen one of these in years," Mrs. Nash said, holding the door for the girls. They climbed up on the red vinyl stools and spun around.

Rebecca's mother read from the menu posted overhead. "Grilled cheese, chili, BLTs. My goodness, corned beef hash—I haven't seen that on a menu for years."

The girls ordered grilled cheese. Mrs. Nash decided on the BLT and Rebecca's mother tried the corned beef hash. After lunch they walked through the neighborhood until it was almost three.

"I'm so excited," Margaret said. She danced a few steps and twirled around. "What part do you want?"

"I don't know," Bea said. "I've never seen *The Nutcracker.*"

"You've never seen it!" Margaret was shocked. "I go every year. It's my Christmas present from my grandmother."

"I've seen it three times," Rebecca said.

"Clara is the best part, of course," Margaret said. "Last year's Clara gave us chocolate lollipops shaped like Christmas trees. Party children are next best. They wear fancy dresses and they have a good dance. Plus they're on stage for a long time. Reindeer are the worst! They wear dumb masks and they hold their hands in front like this." She let her hands droop like a dog begging. "I hope I'm a Chinese dancer or a polichinelle. I was a polichinelle last year. But I think I'm too tall this year."

"I was a baby mouse, because I'm short," Rebecca said. "I wore a fur suit and ran around during the battle scene. I hope I get to do a real dance this year. I grew a lot."

They'd reached the door of the ballet school. "Good luck," Margaret said.

Inside, a lady checked for their names on her clipboard and smiled. "Congratulations," she said. She pointed to the far end of the lobby. A line of tables stretched out across the back of the lobby with letters posted on the wall.

Bea lined up at table M-N-O-P. When she reached the front she told the woman her name and was handed an envelope with her part inside. Bea snaked her way back through the crowd. When she reached her mother she opened the envelope.

"Polichinelle, Cast B," she read aloud.

"Congratulations!" Her mother hugged her. "Let me see the dates for these performances."

"We're the same," Rebecca squealed. "Cast B, too! I've got to find my mother." Rebecca disappeared into the throng of dancers and parents.

Margaret came skittering over, her face shining. She waved the envelope and hopped up and down. "I'm a party child. I can't believe it. I never thought I'd get to be in the party scene."

"Why not?" Bea asked.

"My mother said she's never seen a black child in the party scene. She said the sun will stop in the sky the day a black child plays Clara." Margaret waved the envelope overhead like a flag. "A party child! I can't wait to tell my mom."

"Let's find a phone and you can call her," Mrs. Nash suggested. "What cast are you in?"

"Cast B. I can't reach her now. Her shift is seven to three. I'll tell her when she gets home from the hospital."

"Then let us give you a ride home," Mrs. Nash offered. Margaret agreed.

On the way out they passed children laughing and children in tears, proud mothers, tired mothers, and angry mothers. One very large mother was shouting at the lady in the black leotard. The mother wore a brown fur coat like a grizzly bear. The lady in black was very thin, and the angry mother was so wide that she almost hid her from view. But Bea could tell from the leotard lady's face that she wasn't threatened one bit.

"If you don't like the parts, turn them down," the lady in black said to the bear mother.

"I think that's the twins' mother," Bea whispered. "I saw her at ballet class once."

"I bet she wanted them in the party scene," Margaret hissed.

"They aren't good dancers," Bea whispered. "Why would they get picked to be party children?"

"They're twins and they think they're cute. They think that's all it takes."

Further down the hall, the twins were sitting on a bench, swinging their feet.

"What part did you get?" Margaret asked.

"We don't know yet. Mommy's talking to the casting lady. How about you?"

"I'm a party child," Margaret said. "Bea's a polichinelle."

Bea tugged Margaret's arm. "See you in class," she said to the twins. She pulled Margaret outside. "They look mad enough to spit."

"Too bad," Margaret said. "What can they do?"

"I don't know," Bea said. But the twins' frowns made her shiver. "They're sneaky and dangerous."

"Like snakes?" Margaret asked.

"Meaner than snakes. They're like those fish that eat all the flesh off your bones and leave just your skeleton. Piranhas!"

CHAPTER 7

*R*EHEARSALS

Schedules for *Nutcracker* rehearsals covered the lobby wall at the ballet school. It looked like the timetable at the train station, except instead of men in business suits, girls in leotards stood in front of it every day. Alongside the schedules were notices and frantic requests:

Polichinelle in Cast A needs ride from Smithville. URGENT!

Party child in Cast B wants to trade with Cast A party child.

Reindeer allergic to mask wants to trade roles with Soldier in Cast A. Desperate!

All sixteen polichinelles practiced together, eight from Cast A and eight from Cast B. Most were from levels one and two at the ballet school, with a few girls from other schools. The ones from other schools stood out because of their shiny, bright leotards. One even wore a little skirt with sequins. Bea wondered what Madame would say if she saw that!

A tall man strode into the room clapping his hands. "Okay, okay, peanuts, time to work. My name is James and I am your very own mother. Your Mother Ginger that is. How many of you have seen *The Nutcracker?*"

More than half the group raised their hands.

"Good, so you know who Mother Ginger is. The rest of you listen up." James described the scene. "Mother Ginger is a big lady." He paused and spread his arms wide, and made his eyes wide, too. "She is a *very* big lady. She sashays out to the center of the stage." With his hands at his waist, James wiggled his hips and stepped forward. The polichinelles giggled. "You brats are all hiding under her skirt and you come racing out." He ran around in a circle waving his hands. "And that's how it goes. Now line up and we'll start to learn the steps."

Bea didn't like being called a brat but she lined up with the others. James paired them off by twos, a girl polichinelle and a boy polichinelle. Bea was a boy. The

boys got to turn a cartwheel. Rebecca was her partner.

"Listen up. This is *very* important." James gathered them into a clump around himself. "See these?" He pointed to his feet. "See how big they are? These are nothing compared to Mother Ginger's stompers." James held up a stilt with a huge wooden shoe on the bottom, the size of a cement block. "This is Mother Ginger's foot. When you're under the skirt, can I see you? No! No! No! I don't have X-ray vision. I can't see you down there. I'll be stepping sideways like a crab. You'll be down there under my skirt, crouched over, stepping on tiptoes in little baby steps. Right?"

The polichinelles all nodded.

"So what happens if one silly brat gets in my way?" James paused for effect. "I'll tell you exactly what happens. This!" He stamped the wooden foot down hard on the floor.

The polichinelles jumped back.

James bared his teeth. "Squash! Ouch!" He glared at them one by one. "So stay in your places!"

After rehearsal, when the girls jumped into the Nashes' car, Bea was still simmering. "Mother Ginger is mean. He's rotten," she told her mother. "He's not a good teacher at all. He yelled and tried to scare us."

"I'm sure it's no picnic working with a bunch of giggling girls. He probably wishes he was one of the Russian dancers."

"It's not our fault that he got this part," Rebecca said. "He doesn't have to be such a grump."

Whenever the party children rehearsed at the same

time as the polichinelles, Mrs. Nash gave Margaret a ride home. "I watched Margaret at rehearsal tonight," Mrs. Nash told Bea after they had dropped Margaret off. "She was absolutely the best of all of them. What long legs! Honestly, she was better than the girl playing Clara."

"I wonder why they didn't choose her for Clara?" Bea said.

CHAPTER 8

A MEAN TRICK

On Sunday afternoon, Bea played street hockey with Pete and other neighborhood boys. She wasn't as quick as she'd been when she played more often. She'd lost the knack of getting a shot off fast.

Peter reassured her. "You're just rusty. It will come back." He kept passing to her and she finally scored.

"That felt great," Bea crowed.

"See what you're missing?" Pete said. "Why do you have to dance so much?"

Bea didn't try to explain. Pete wouldn't believe her if she said ballet was as much fun as hockey. But there were times when the music and the steps fit together so well that she just moved and it came out right. That was more fun than anything.

"My dad's making an ice rink in our backyard this year," Pete said. "He already bought the plastic and the wood for the edges. As soon as it gets below freezing, he'll start layering the ice. He's going to try to put lines in the ice like a real rink. We can have a tournament over Christmas vacation."

"I have *Nutcracker* performances," Bea reminded him.

"That stinks!" Pete said. Then he added, "You can make some of the games when you're not dancing, can't you?"

"I hope so," said Bea. "Are you coming to see the ballet?"

Pete nodded. "My mom got the tickets already. We're going with your family."

"Promise you won't laugh if I drop my partner? I'm supposed to catch her when she falls back but she does it wrong and her feet slip out too much. Yesterday I dropped her twice."

"Cool!" said Pete. "Can you do it on purpose?"

At ballet class on Monday, the twins arrived in the dressing room too late to get their usual spot near the mirror. They had to use the bench by the window where Bea and Margaret were changing. Bea knew they weren't polichinelles because she hadn't seen them at rehearsal. Margaret had told her they weren't party children.

"What part did you get in *The Nutcracker?*" she asked Caitlin, the twin with freckles.

"We're angels," Caitlin said.

"It's a dumb dance," said Erin. "We take stupid baby steps and go in a circle."

"Better than being a soldier," Margaret said. She demonstrated the stiff-legged steps with a scowl that made Bea laugh.

"I don't know why they chose you for the party scene," Caitlin said to Margaret.

"Mommy said you must know someone in the company," Erin added. "That's the only way you could have gotten that part."

"What are you talking about?" Bea said, outraged. "Margaret's the best dancer here. Your mother's a nutmom."

"If she's so good, then why isn't she Clara?" Erin sneered.

Bea didn't have an answer for that. Margaret tugged her hand. "It's time for class."

"You'll never be Clara," Erin said. "Clara's *white,* in case you haven't noticed."

Bea whirled around to face the twins. "If you two can be angels, anyone can be anything!"

Bea ran to catch up with Margaret. "I hope they're in Cast A. Angels! Whoever gave them that role sure didn't know them!"

Margaret looked glum. Bea wished she could make her smile. It was so unlike Margaret to be unhappy at ballet.

In class Madame taught a new combination, a tricky mix of tempos, slow, then fast, then slow again. Bea concentrated hard, trying to match the steps to the music. The first time, Bea muddled the steps in the middle and ended up lagging behind her partners. As they waited for the next turn, she remembered to count the beats the way Margaret had shown her. Da, *dum,* da, da, wait. Da, *dum,* da, da. Then the fast part: *dum, dum,* da, *dum, dum,* da. Bea kept repeating it as other trios danced. On her second trip across the floor, murmuring the beats helped her fit the steps to the music. Madame smiled and nodded. "Ah, Bea-ah-treesse. Excellent, excellent, *ma chérie.*"

Erin stuck her tongue out as Bea passed her.

The twins were still bungling the steps at the end of class. "It's too hard," Erin whined.

"Concentrate, *ma petite.* It will come."

"Blah, blah, blah, blah," Erin mimicked to her twin as they strutted back to the dressing room. "Stupid old crow."

Bea dawdled on purpose to avoid sharing a bench with the twins again. She stopped for a drink at the water fountain and peered in a window at the advanced class. The older girls wore toe shoes. The ribbons crisscrossed around their ankles, and the toes had hard flat fronts, making a small surface to stand on. Bea watched them rise up on their toes, turn, then cross the room in little steps, the hard toes tapping on the floor. Someday I'll do that, she thought. I wonder if it hurts to go up on your toes. She'd heard from Margaret that dancers wrapped their toes in soft lamb's wool to cushion them. She stayed at the window watching until the class finished the routine.

When she reached the dressing room, the twins had vanished, and Margaret was already gone, too. Bea started to change into her jeans and sneakers. But her sneakers weren't in her bag. She looked in the cubby where she'd stuffed her jacket, but no sneakers!

"Have you seen any sneakers?" she asked the few dancers still changing.

"There's a pair in the bathroom," an older girl told her. "I figured someone had spilled something and had to wash them out."

It took Bea a few seconds to spot them, slung over the bar of the stall, dripping water. A puddle had formed beneath them. Bea jumped three times before she grabbed the toe of one sneaker and pulled them down. She landed right in the puddle, so her tights got wet, too. Unable to think of a better plan, she pulled the wet shoes on over the wet tights and squished out to the curb where her mother was waiting.

"Who would do a thing like that?" Mrs. Nash asked.

Bea shrugged, but she knew exactly who had done it.

CHAPTER 9

$\mathcal{M}$ARGARET TO
THE $\mathcal{R}$ESCUE

For the next month, ballet classes and rehearsals took up four afternoons a week. No wonder the music from *The Nutcracker* played in Bea's head over and over again.

"I feel like I'm dancing in my sleep," she told her mother.

"Chin up, Bumblebee," Mrs. Nash said. "Once the performances start, you'll be happy you did it."

At ballet class, Bea tried to ignore the twins, but it was hard.

"B is for baby," Caitlin whispered during warmups. "Baby and brat."

"Nash-ty," Erin added with a mean giggle.

Bea asked her mother to buy a combination lock for the dressing-room lockers. She stuffed Margaret's bag inside as well as her own. "Don't leave any of your things around," she warned. "I don't trust those two. It took three days for my sneakers to dry."

Luckily the twins were in a different scene, so Bea didn't see them at rehearsals. The polichinelles worked hard at first. But practicing the dance over and over was boring. So they played games right under Mother Ginger's nose!

Bea liked Pinch Tag the best. The game started by one dancer pinching someone nearby and whispering, "You're it. No backs." Whoever was It tried to pinch someone else during the dance. The trick was to wait until another polichinelle danced by, then pinch her without missing a step and without James noticing.

Grumpy James! His temper flared up as fast as kindling. The polichinelles all giggled when James exploded. His face flushed and his thick eyebrows jumped. He yelled, too—loud! The first time it happened Bea cringed, but soon she laughed softly with the others.

"I love it when he roars," Rebecca whispered as they danced arm in arm. "He looks so funny."

Bea whispered back, "He hates us."

The last week of rehearsals, James wore his costume: stilts with giant black shoes on the ends; the huge ruffled skirt covering a wood and wire structure; bosoms as big as pumpkins. Perched up high, James wore a frizzy red wig and bonnet, with circles of red on his cheeks and a wart on his chin. He looked so ugly!

As the rehearsals dragged on, James grew even grumpier. "Watch me," he told the polichinelles. When the music started, James stepped sideways across the floor on his stilts, his wide skirt swaying from side to side like a ship on waves.

"If you trip me and I fall over, you get buried inside this thing." He thumped on the structure beneath the skirt. "Stay in place or it's your funeral and I won't be the one crying."

Bea shuddered at the thought of Mother Ginger falling. The skirt would crash like a tree, trapping the polichinelles inside while Mother Ginger's stilts and feet thrashed. Bea vowed to be very careful. No games underneath the skirt, she told herself.

James grouped them in a tight formation on either side of his stilts. "These are your spots. Don't forget them. Don't step in front of me, *understand?*"

Bea clenched her fists and waited for the music. Overhead, his voice muffled by the skirt, James counted, "One, two, three." Then the skirt began its seasick swaying. Underneath the polichinelles crouched and took baby steps as Mother Ginger edged out to the middle of the floor. Then James opened the panel and let them out.

Bea gulped fresh air as soon as she cleared the flap of the skirt. Polichinelles took their positions and the happy dance began. Bea's favorite part came when the girl polichinelles curtsied and the boy polichinelles turned cartwheels. Bea kept her legs straight and far apart like the spokes of a wheel.

Only one moment in the dance worried her. Toward the end she stood behind Rebecca and caught her as she fell backward, kicking one foot up. If the girl polichinelle kept her body stiff, her partner could easily push her. But Rebecca sagged so much her fanny practically touched the floor. Bea struggled to hold her. Getting her up on her feet required a mighty shove. Sometimes Rebecca slipped through Bea's hands and landed on the floor.

"You dropped me," Rebecca accused.

"You fell," Bea retorted.

"You're supposed to catch me," Rebecca argued.

"You're not supposed to fall. Don't go back so far."

They argued and argued.

"If she'd just stay more upright, I could do it," Bea complained to Margaret after class the next day. "But she sags like a rag doll and she's too heavy to hold. She won't listen to me."

"It sounds like she doesn't understand the step. Ask James to show her what she's doing wrong," Margaret suggested.

Bea shook her head. "All James does is yell. He thinks I'm dropping her on purpose for a joke. Some joke! I don't want everyone to laugh at me!"

Margaret was thoughtful while she buttoned her sweater. "Do you have rehearsal tomorrow?" she asked. Bea nodded. "Me, too," Margaret said. "If I finish first, I'll come and watch the dance and see if I can figure out what's going wrong. I can't promise anything," she cautioned. But when Bea's frown returned, she added, "We'll fix it. You won't drop her."

Caitlin stuck her head out from behind a row of lockers where she'd been eavesdropping. "Bea-ah-treesse Butterfingers! I know you'll screw up. I can't wait. We'll be watching and laughing. I bet you drop your partner right on her butt and she cries in front of everyone. You'll wreck the dance." She cackled. "Hey Erin, wait till you hear this!" she called to her twin, and slipped away to the other side of the dressing room.

"She's probably right," Bea sighed.

"Leave it to me," Margaret said. "Don't listen to those devil twins!" She shook her fist.

"Devil twins!" Bea's face brightened. "Devil twins in the angel scene."

Bea tried to keep worried thoughts out of her mind, but at night, as she tried to sleep, she pictured the whole disaster: Rebecca slipping between her arms and lying on her back with her feet in the air; James pointing down at her from high up on his stilts, a glare on his face.

The next day, Margaret slipped in through the back door toward the end of rehearsal. After James dismissed the group, Bea and Rebecca huddled with Margaret. The room cleared in a few minutes. "Now show me the dance," Margaret said.

Margaret hummed the music while Bea and Rebecca did the skips, the turn, the patty-cake hand claps and then the falling back move. Rebecca flopped backward off balance while Bea struggled to hold her up.

"Now try it with me," Margaret said.

Bea stood behind again and Margaret leaned backward a little, but she kept both feet on the ground and bent her knees. "Put your hands under my arms now so I can lean back further. See, I've got my weight on my right foot. I can kick my left foot up without losing my balance or falling." Margaret demonstrated and Bea pushed her upright easily. "Now you try it with me," Margaret told Rebecca. "Don't let your middle bend. It just pulls you down."

They practiced it again and again with Margaret coaching Rebecca to keep her weight forward and how far back to lean. Finally Rebecca could do the step gracefully.

"Thanks, Margaret," Bea said. "You're a good friend."

"A good dancer and a good friend," Rebecca added.

That week, the temperature dropped below freezing every night. Friday at school Pete asked Bea, "Want to come over for dinner and skate afterward?"

At Pete's zany house toys were strewn everywhere. Pete's mom let the kids turn the dining-room table into a fort and eat snacks like marshmallow fluff sandwiches and strawberry syrup in milk. Pete's little brothers scooted through the rooms like race cars, knocking against furniture, tumbling and skidding. Their mother just laughed as if this was all a circus and her sons were clowns sent to entertain her.

At Friday dinner the children ate spaghetti at the kitchen table. Ryan, the three-year-old, used his hands, while Timmy, who was four, slurped up the strands noisily.

At Bea's house the dining-room table was always set with a tablecloth and candles. The family sat down all together, Bea, Andy, and their mom and dad. No TV and no books at the table. "We like to see you. It's the one calm time in the whole day when we have a chance to hear about each other's lives," Mrs. Nash said.

Dinner at Pete's was never calm, but it was fun. The meal ended as soon as the youngest popped off his chair, unable to keep still any longer. Bea helped Pete clear the dishes and wipe the table off before they put on their skates.

Outside the rink gleamed in the light from the kitchen window. Bea glided out and circled the rink, shaking out her legs and stretching overhead with her stick between her hands. Pete did knee bends and then sped up, sprinting from end to end. "What should we name our team?" he asked when he pulled up beside her.

At first all Bea could think of were names from *The Nutcracker*: reindeer, snowflakes, the mouse king. She knew better than to suggest these to Pete. "How about the Icicles?" she said. "Or the Glaciers?"

"Glaciers," Pete said. "The ice men. That's good."

Soon four more boys and two girls showed up: four on a team. The night air stung Bea's cheeks as the wind whipped over the ice. She caught a pass on the end of her stick and shot at the net so fast that the goalie wasn't even looking in the right direction. "Score!" Bea cried.

Pete slapped her palm with his glove. "I told you the knack would come back."

CHAPTER 10

OPENING NIGHT

"First performance tonight! Excited?" Mrs. Nash asked Bea at breakfast. "Remind me what time you have to get to the theater."

"Six o'clock," Bea said, stirring her cocoa.

"Why so early?" her mother asked.

"We get our costumes and the makeup ladies put on our lipstick and powder and stuff."

"Good luck, sweetheart," her father said, tousling her hair. "Break a leg!"

"Dad!" Bea protested.

"That means good luck in the theater. I figured it's the same for ballet," he said.

After school, Bea raced through her homework and then changed into a white leotard and tights for her costume. Mrs. Nash persuaded her to eat a bowl of soup and half a tuna sandwich before leaving. At the theater the doorman checked for Bea's name on the cast list and buzzed open the door for her. She was so excited that she forgot to kiss her mother good-bye, so she blew her a kiss through the glass.

Bea spotted three other polichinelles at the foot of the stairs and hurried to catch up with them. "This way, girls," called a woman in a smock. "Put your coats in a locker and get on your ballet shoes."

Another lady in a smock handed Bea the white silk pants she'd tried on at dress rehearsal. The pant legs were short and much wider than any pants Bea had ever worn.

"Perfect," said the wardrobe lady. "We don't want you tripping, do we?" She buttoned Bea into her white jacket with red trim around the collar and handed her the funny white hat that reminded Bea of a big boat. The hat had an elastic that went under her chin. Good thing, or I'd lose it when I turn my cartwheel, Bea thought.

The makeup ladies frowned all the time. One was tall and one was short. The short one sat Bea in front of the mirror. She spread makeup over Bea's face, darkened her eyebrows, brushed pink on her cheeks, and put on lipstick. Then she powdered Bea's face all over lightly with a powder puff the size of a pie plate. "Don't put a finger on this, understand? No eating or drinking, either. If you smudge this face, I have to start all over again and I have no time for such nonsense." Bea escaped from the chair.

Costumed children clustered on the other side of the room, far away from the grouchy smock ladies. Party children wore satin dresses or velvet suits with lace collars that looked itchy. The Chinese dancers' silk jackets were embroidered with dragons. Angels drifted around holding up the hems of their long white robes. Reindeer and baby mice carried their masks under their arms. Dancers with full skirts twirled around and around, seeing how far their skirts swung out in circles. Bea spotted Margaret twirling with the others, her green dress shining like a Christmas ornament.

"I can't decide if you look like the princess or the pea," Bea teased.

"I'm a princess and you are my jester," Margaret said and dipped a deep curtsy. Bea bowed in return, just the way she did in her dance. Rebecca came skipping over with a pack of cards in her hand. "Want to play?" she asked.

Bea spotted the twins in their white gowns and gold halos playing tag near the door. She nudged Margaret. "I didn't know they were in Cast B," she whispered. Margaret rolled her eyes. Two reindeer from their ballet class joined the game. They all had to stand up so their costumes wouldn't wrinkle.

Soon the party children were called for their scene and the reindeer had to line up by size. That finished the game, so Bea and Rebecca practiced their falling backward step a few times without any trouble. When the angels were called for their scene, Bea watched the twins leave with a feeling of relief. She wasn't sure what mischief they could do here in front of so many grown-ups, but if they could find a way, they'd make trouble. Bea was sure of that, just as she knew that James would be a grouch tonight.

Finally it was almost time for Mother Ginger's appearance. The children ducked under the skirt. It was dark and stuffy inside. James, grumpy as usual, snarled, "Stay in your places, brats." The music began and James counted, "One, two, three, *now.*" Hunched over with her hands on her knees, Bea took baby steps forward. The audience laughed when they first glimpsed Mother Ginger's huge skirt and then her painted face and curly wig.

Maybe it was the laughter that made the polichinelle up in front forget her place. Maybe she had first-night jitters. She might have drifted out of place by just a bit, just one step sideways. No one knew exactly what happened under the big skirt.

Suddenly Ellie shrieked with pain. Mother Ginger lurched from side to side. For a moment, Bea thought Mother Ginger would topple over. But James regained his balance and gradually the big skirt stopped its wild rocking.

"Oh, my foot! Ow, ow. He stepped on my foot," Ellie moaned softly. Bea could tell she was crying.

The orchestra kept playing and James hissed down, "Out you go." The skirt flap opened, and two by two, polichinelles skipped onto the stage. Ellie skip-hopped and struggled to keep up with her partner, skip, hop, skip, hop.

Bea concentrated on the dance and tried to remember to smile. Please, please don't let me drop Rebecca, she whispered to herself. Skip, turn, patty-cake, twirl, then the step. Rebecca kept her back straight and Bea held her for the kick, pushing her upright with just a tiny shove. Perfect!

The polichinelles scurried back under Mother Ginger's skirt at the end of their dance. The audience applauded as the giant woman sashayed offstage. She paused for a minute as one polichinelle darted out to wave a last good-bye at the audience.

Backstage, dancers clustered around Ellie, who was rubbing her foot with both hands. Tears streaked her makeup. James unhinged the skirt and clumped over with Mother Ginger's stilts still strapped on to his feet. "I warned you to stay in position. Lucky for all of us I didn't fall over."

Ellie nodded, still rubbing her foot.

"You got through the whole dance, though. That takes guts. Good job, kid," James said. "Sorry I mashed your foot. Does it still hurt?"

Ellie nodded, but smiled at James's compliment.

"Get the kid some ice," James ordered the makeup ladies.

By the end of the act when the polichinelles were due back onstage, Ellie was grinning.

After the show, Bea and her family had dinner at a restaurant with Pete and his parents. Mrs. Nash showed Bea her name in the program: *Beatrice Nash*.

"I want your autograph," Pete said. Bea signed his program on the page where her name was printed.

During dinner, Bea told the story of Mother Ginger and poor Ellie's squashed foot.

"I hope that will be the only calamity," Mr. Nash said. "Sometimes trouble comes in threes. Show business people are superstitious."

"I don't think anything else will go wrong," Bea said.

"I hope not," Mr. Nash said.

CHAPTER 11

$\mathcal{F}$ALLEN $\mathcal{A}$NGELS

Bea couldn't forget her father's words: trouble comes in threes. She kept waiting for a dancer to miss a cue or fall. At the Wednesday matinee, as a special treat, the polichinelles were allowed to watch Act I. Bea sat in the front row of the balcony where she could lean forward and stare right down at the stage. The lights dimmed and the music began. Bea entered the scene before her completely, as if she were inside a dream. When the Christmas tree began to grow and grow and grow, she gasped.

Rebecca, sitting beside her, giggled and whispered, "You didn't know that was going to happen, did you?"

Just before the polichinelles had to go down to get

ready for their dance, snowflakes drifted gently onto the stage and settled on dark fir trees. Ballerinas in white tutus twirled and dipped, as light as the snow. The ballerinas gliding among the dark trees and sparkling flakes made Bea sigh with pleasure.

The whole week of Cast B's performance, Bea stayed up past her bedtime. On Friday, she was so tired that she dozed off in the classroom reading corner. Her teacher let her nap until lunchtime. "Rise and shine," she said. "You slept right through math. Did you dream about numbers or nutcrackers?"

Bea shook her head and rubbed her eyes. "I didn't dream at all," she said.

"You didn't snore," Pete reassured her. "You didn't even drool. My father always drools when he falls asleep on the couch."

Backstage that evening, Bea played cards with Margaret and Rebecca. The twins came and stood nearby, watching. Slowly they inched closer and closer until they stood on either side of Margaret, trapping her.

"Is this satin?" Caitlin asked, fingering a fold of Margaret's skirt.

Margaret nodded.

"Who ties your bow?" Erin asked. She picked up the end of the sash.

"The wardrobe lady. Please don't touch it," Margaret said. She stepped away, trying to put distance between the twins and herself. Erin kept hold of the sash and the bow unraveled. Margaret groaned.

"You did that on purpose," Bea said. "Now she'll have to go back to the wardrobe lady. You know she'll get scolded."

"Ohhh, I'm sorry," Erin gushed with phony regret.

"Poor little party girl," Caitlin oozed. "At least her dress isn't torn."

"Is that your next trick?" Bea gave Caitlin a push. As the twin struggled to keep her balance, her heel caught the hem of her robe. *R-I-I-I-P!* The gold trim on the edge of her costume came free.

"Ohhh, I'm so sorry!" Bea said, mimicking Erin's phony regret. "I guess you'll have to get the wardrobe lady to sew it up."

Caitlin glared at her. "You did *that* on purpose."

"You're the one who stepped backward. You've got to be careful with your costume. Better hurry and get it fixed."

"No one will see it with the clouds on the floor," Erin reassured her sister.

"You might trip," Rebecca warned. "You should get it sewn before your scene."

The twins huddled together in the corner, examining the damaged robe and whispering. Bea didn't see them after that.

"Think I'll get in trouble?" Bea asked Rebecca.

"What for? She stepped on her own costume," Rebecca said. "What goes around comes around. That's what my granny always says."

"Just like our dance," Bea said. "We go around and come around."

Soon Margaret returned with her sash freshly tied.

"The costume lady didn't even yell."

Just then the stage manager called the dancers for the party scene. Margaret gave a little wave. "Have fun," she said and skipped away to join the other party children.

At the beginning of the second act, Bea and the other polichinelles waited for Mother Ginger's music. The angels lined up on the other side of the stage.

The music for the angels' dance drifted backstage. It was a sweet melody with harps and a choir of ladies singing. The angels moved one behind the other in a procession, carrying tiny lights while a cloud of stage fog swirled over the floor of the stage. It was usually a tranquil scene, but tonight, halfway through the dance, a loud crash stopped the music.

Bea couldn't see the stage. Trouble comes in threes, her father had said. Was this number two?

A ballerina hurried by. "Big angel pileup. One tripped and they fell like dominoes. Fallen angels everywhere."

The music started up again and the dance continued.

The polichinelles twittered under Mother Ginger's skirt like birds in a bush. What happened? Was anyone hurt? Whose fault was it?

Bea was silent. Maybe it was the ripped hem.

All around her the polichinelles whispered, until James hissed, "Quiet, brats! If you don't shut up, I'm going to *fart!*"

That silenced them. Being stuck under the skirt with James's smelly gas was a horrible thought.

Mother Ginger's music began. James sidestepped on stage and the skirt swayed from side to side. Everyone stayed in position, skipped out, and took their places without a misstep. The patty-cakes and cartwheels went well. Bea caught Rebecca and pushed her upright. From the first skip to the last wave, the dance was perfect.

Backstage, the polichinelles found the angels sitting on the floor, still wearing their leotards and tights. A few held ice packs on their ankles. The stage manager stood above them with his hands on his hips. "The director will meet with all of you angels after the final curtain. He's quite upset. A New York critic was in the theater tonight and he didn't come all the way up here to see a bunch of girls scattered all over the stage like bowling pins."

As Bea tiptoed past she snuck a look at Caitlin and Erin. They sat with chins in their hands, staring at the floor. Bea wasn't sure, but she thought Caitlin was crying. Her shoulders heaved every so often, from sobs or hiccups.

All through the final scene Bea worried that the twins would blame her for the accident. Her tears blurred the giant balloon that carried Clara and the prince high above the stage. She blinked them back before they could roll down her cheeks.

When the curtain dropped, she slipped ahead of the other dancers and quickly turned in her costume, running upstairs without pausing to speak to anyone.

"Oh, Mom," she sobbed as she collapsed onto the car

seat. She blurted out the whole story: the sash, the torn hem, the angels' catastrophe. "Do you think I'll get punished?" Bea asked. She hiccuped again.

"Maybe I'm missing something," Ms. Nash said. "Caitlin should have gotten her costume fixed. It's not clear that's what caused the mess anyway. It's too bad it happened, but I don't think it's your fault." She gave Bea a one-armed hug. "You're shivering! Let's get you into a bath, pronto."

At home, lying in a tub scented with her mother's lavender bath salts, Bea closed her eyes and sank down so the hot water was up to her chin. Angels toppling like bowling pins! She could imagine the scene: the clouds, the lights, sweet music, white gowns, and gold halos. Then crash—all fall down. What would Pete say when she told him?

She described it to him the next day when they were skating.

"I wish I'd seen that," he said. "Did the audience laugh? Think they fell like this?" He dove onto the ice, belly down.

"You look like a penguin," Bea said.

Pete groaned. "When is this dumb *Nutcracker* over?"

"Soon," Bea said.

"Good!" Pete said. "Maybe when it's finished, the Glaciers can win a few games."

CHAPTER 12
MARGARET'S TURN

Sunday morning Bea didn't wake up until Bigfoot slipped through her door and jumped up beside her. He nestled in, kneading the blanket with his snowshoe paws. Bea scratched between his ears and started him purring.

"Want to be in the ballet, Bigfoot? You could be Mother Ginger with your big paws," Bea told the cat. "But you'd hate the skirt."

Bigfoot yawned, showing his pink tongue and white teeth.

"You want another part? How about the Mouse King? He's got gray fur."

Bigfoot arched his back in a stretch. He jumped off the bed and padded out of the room with his tail curled high above his back.

"Don't like that part either?" Bea laughed.

The sleet streaming down the window canceled Bea's plan to skate with Pete. Instead, after breakfast, Pete came over and they settled down in the living room with the Sorry game box.

"Can I play?" Andy asked.

"If you make us some cocoa first," Bea bargained.

"I'm not your slave," Andy said.

"Do you want to play or not?" Bea asked.

"Fine! I'll do it," Andy said. "Don't start without me."

While they were waiting for Andy, Mr. Nash poked his head in. "If you two bring some logs up from the basement, I'll build a fire in the fireplace." Soon they had a fire and cocoa to warm them.

"Don't cheat, Andy. Count the spaces right," Bea warned.

"I don't cheat," Andy protested. "I make mistakes."

"Mistakes on purpose," Bea said. "Be careful. I'm counting."

Andy won the first game fairly. Halfway through the second game, music from *The Nutcracker* came on the radio.

Bea groaned. "I am *so* tired of that music."

Pete jumped up, grabbed the poker from the fireplace, and waved it through the air as a sword. Not wanting to be outdone, Andy leaped up on the couch.

"I'll be the main mouse. I need a sword, too."

"You better put the poker back before you hit some-thing," Bea warned.

"We can use pretend swords," Pete said. "Or we can make them out of cardboard."

"Bea, you can be the girl," Andy said. "Run around like you're scared."

"No way!" Bea said. "I'll be the magician." She looked around the room. "I need a cape. Let's find costumes."

"I'm not wearing tights," Andy said, still jumping on the couch. He clutched the waist of his sweatpants as if someone might pull them down.

Upstairs they poked in closets and piled up possibilities: Mr. Nash's den leader's shirt; a cape from an old Halloween costume; Andy's plastic knight's sword.

Back in the living room they pushed back the chairs to make more room.

"We've even got a Christmas tree, just like in the ballet," Andy said.

"Imagine if the tree went right through the ceiling," Bea said. "It would be in Mom and Dad's bedroom."

"I'd like to have a tree in my room," Andy said.

"That's because you're a monkey," Bea teased. Andy threw a couch pillow at her, just missing a brass lamp.

Before the matinee performance, and afterward, on Sunday evening, Bea worked on her Christmas presents. She'd woven a bookmark for her mother. For Andy she'd made a book of jokes and funny drawings. She'd bought six handkerchiefs for her father and was cross-stitching his initials in the corner of each one. By Monday morning, she had finished two and was just starting the third handkerchief when the telephone rang.

As soon as Bea said, "Hello," Margaret's words tumbled out so fast that Bea couldn't keep up. "Hold on," Bea said. "Start over and slow down!"

"I'm going to be Clara. Tomorrow!" Margaret explained that the Cast B Clara had the flu and the Clara from Cast A was out of town for the holiday. "They picked me. Can you believe it?"

"Of course I believe it," Bea said.

"I know Clara's party scene dance from all the rehearsals. In the battle all she does is run around and throw her slipper at the Mouse King. Act Two's easy. Clara just sits on the throne." Margaret paused to catch her breath. "They gave me a tape to watch and I have to go in tomorrow morning and rehearse all day. Can you come and sleep over? Please please please please? We can watch the tape together and practice."

Bea ran to tell her mother the news.

"That's wonderful!" Mrs. Nash said. "Now everyone will see Margaret dance! Get your things together and I'll drive you right over."

Margaret must have been watching for the car from

her living-room window. She ran downstairs to open the door before Bea reached the front porch. Mrs. Nash gave Margaret a big hug.

"Congratulations, Superstar. I can just imagine how lovely you'll look."

"You don't have to imagine. My mom has a ticket for you. Will you come?"

"I'd drive through a blizzard to see this. Thank your mother and tell her I'm thrilled." Mrs. Nash gave Bea a kiss. "Have fun, Bumblebee."

The girls settled on the rug in front of the television set. Margaret stretched her legs in a wide V. "They taped Cast A this year," Margaret said. "See how all the scenery and costumes are the same as in our performances?"

"Isn't *The Nutcracker* always the same?" Bea asked.

Margaret shook her head. "Every year something's new. This year Drosselmeyer's cape is purple. I think it makes him look more like a magician."

The magician had long skinny legs and arms and wore a black patch over one eye. He swirled his purple cape in an arc of shiny satin and a gift magically appeared in his hand.

"He looks like a spider except for the cape," Bea said.

"Here comes Clara's dance with Drosselmeyer. This is the part I have to learn," Margaret said.

They watched carefully. Then Margaret rewound the tape and they watched again. Margaret jumped up and tried several steps. "Let's do this. We'll watch the dance and then you push pause after each section and I'll copy the steps I just saw."

Bea held the remote control with one finger on Pause. After every section of the dance, she pushed the button and stopped the dancers in midstep. Margaret mimicked the dance, freezing in the same position. "It's like playing Statues," she laughed, trying to balance with one foot off the ground and an arm overhead.

Finally, Margaret put the steps together from Drosselmeyer's first bow to Clara's final curtsy. Then she flopped on the sofa. "I'm not so nervous now. With rehearsals tomorrow, I should be okay."

In the morning, Bea wished Margaret good luck. "I won't say break a leg. I hate it when they say that. Imagine if it really happened."

Margaret nodded. "I heard about a dancer who injured her foot halfway through a ballet. The understudy was sitting out front in the audience. They found her and had her change at intermission. She finished the ballet in place of the other famous ballerina. And she became a star!"

"You're the star tonight," Bea said.

Bea sat out front in an orchestra seat while Margaret rehearsed her scenes with Drosselmeyer and the Nutcracker Prince. They practiced the same dances again and again. Luckily, Bea had her embroidery to do, or she would have been very bored. After lunch, all the dancers in Act I assembled for a full run-through.

The dancing in the first act was perfect. Margaret's face

shone with pleasure. When she and Drosselmeyer danced their duet, she turned without a wobble. Drosselmeyer lifted her overhead with ease. At the end of the party scene, the director himself came onstage clapping. "Good job," he said, patting Margaret on the back.

In the next scene Margaret was alone onstage, asleep in a bed with a white coverlet. She awakened, turned back the covers, and stepped down onto the stage in her white nightgown. The stage was dark except for the spotlight shining on her. Margaret looked so small and fragile as she tiptoed across the stage that Bea held her breath.

The battle started. Huge mice with big bellies scurried back and forth across the stage, running in circles and bumping stomachs. They were so silly it was impossible to be afraid of them. The Nutcracker Prince and the Mouse King had a sword fight. Then Clara threw her slipper. It hit the Mouse King and down he fell with his feet up in the air, the mound of his belly as round as an igloo. The mice brought a stretcher and they lifted the Mouse King onto it. But when they picked it up, one side was too low and the Mouse King slipped right off.

"Do it over," the director ordered.

So again the mice brought out the stretcher and tried to carry the king offstage. But he slipped off! The third time, the stretcher still wasn't straight. When he fell again, the Mouse King stood up, waved his fist at the other mice, and carried the stretcher off himself. The dancers onstage laughed and clapped as the king disappeared into the wings.

CHAPTER 13

A New Clara

After the rehearsal, Bea and Margaret went for supper. Margaret's mother and her grandmother waited outside the stage door, wrapped in wool coats and woven shawls. Mrs. Nash hurried up to the group and was introduced to Margaret's grandmother.

"What incredible shawls!" she said. "The colors remind me of the sky and the sea."

"Margaret's aunt, Sarah, is the weaver," her grandmother said. "She lives on the West Coast so she can't be here tonight. These are our Christmas presents. She made one for Margaret, too, in silver and gold. You can tell who's the star in Sarah's eyes."

Mrs. Nash led the group to a small café that smelled of coffee and chocolate. The waitress took their orders and quickly returned with steaming bowls of soup and sandwiches. Outside, shoppers bent their heads into the wind. Bea nudged Margaret. "It looks like the opening scene where everyone hurries across the stage, all bundled up and carrying presents."

"Soon the man with the Christmas tree will come out and then Drosselmeyer," Margaret said.

"You know every bit of this ballet, don't you?" Mrs. Nash said with a smile.

"She's seen it many times," Margaret's grandmother said. "But tonight will be the best performance of all." She squeezed Margaret's hand. "We are so proud of you," she said.

When they were finished, the girls walked back to the theater to change. The grown-ups relaxed in the café, enjoying their coffee and dessert.

Margaret and Bea hurried through the stage door and down the stairs. As soon as they reached the dressing room, a costume lady led Margaret off to get dressed for her new role. Margaret waved good-bye to Bea. She looked nervous.

"Don't worry!" Bea called after her.

Bea changed into her polichinelle suit and joined the other children who were playing cards and skipping around the way they did every night. They don't even know there's a new Clara tonight, Bea thought. She found Rebecca in the crowd.

"Did you hear about Margaret?" Bea said.

"What about her?" Rebecca asked. "Where is she?" A child they'd never seen before twirled in Margaret's green party dress. "Who's that?" Rebecca said. "What's she doing in Margaret's dress?"

"Margaret's wearing another dress tonight," Bea said.

"Why?" Rebecca was confused. "I like her green dress."

"Her new dress is white with a blue sash," Bea hinted. "A white dress for the party, then a white nightgown."

"What are you talking about?" Rebecca said. "She probably wears pajamas. I do."

"Rebecca!" Bea said. "Think! Who wears a white party dress and a white nightgown in *The Nutcracker?*"

"Clara does," Rebecca said. Her eyes widened as she understood Bea's clues. "Margaret is Clara?"

Bea nodded.

Just then Margaret came into the room wearing Clara's party dress. Children surrounded her, asking questions.

Margaret waved her hands to quiet everyone. "Yes, I'm playing Clara tonight. The regular Clara has the flu and the Cast A Clara is away for Christmas." She twirled around once, showing the dress. Her skin glowed against the white lace trim. A crown of tiny white flowers nestled in her dark curls. Everyone clapped and said congratulations and good luck. Everyone except the twins.

Bea spotted them standing off to the side. They looked

as if they had been sucking on lemons. While Bea watched, they whispered in each other's ears.

They're plotting something, Bea thought. But what could they do with so many grown-ups around? Just in case, Bea stood near Margaret until she went onstage. Just to be safe.

At the end of the performance, Margaret had an extra bow with the Nutcracker Prince. The director came backstage afterward.

"Wonderful job, my dear," he said, kissing her hand. "Thank you for stepping in when we needed you."

"I'm glad I had the chance," Margaret said.

"That's the spirit," the director said. Then he called out to everyone. "Cast party tomorrow after the last performance. Then we can all relax and enjoy a well-earned vacation."

Bea changed and waited for Margaret. They climbed the stairs to the stage door together. "Was it scary?" Bea asked.

"It was easier than rehearsal. I almost forgot we were onstage," Margaret said. "But you know when I'm all alone on the stage, asleep? And I wake up and the tree grows and the mice come in? Even though I knew it was pretend, it felt scary. The stage is so big and the lights are turned down." Margaret shivered and then laughed at herself. "But the rest was easy."

Margaret's mother and grandmother were waiting at the stage door holding bouquets of roses. They piled them into her arms and each kissed a cheek.

"Seeing you on that stage was the proudest moment of my life," her grandmother said, her eyes shining with happy tears.

Mrs. Nash set a chocolate soldier on top of the flowers.

Margaret thanked them all. "See you tomorrow," she said to Bea. "Thanks for helping me practice."

"Sleep well," Mrs. Nash said.

"I will!" Margaret answered.

On the ride home, the warm air from the heater made Bea drowsy. She fell asleep in the car and hardly woke up when her mother led her upstairs and put her to bed.

CHAPTER 14

*D*EVILS IN THE *W*INGS

Christmas Eve matinee was the last *Nutcracker* performance for the season. The cast children were more excited than ever. The dressing room became a giant game of tag. Soldiers chased reindeer. Baby mice hid behind the skirts of party children. Chinese dancers turned cartwheels and demonstrated splits. Even the wardrobe and makeup ladies smiled as they looked at the games.

"I bet they're glad it's the last day," Bea said to Rebecca as they paused by the wall to catch their breath.

"No more nutkids until next year," Rebecca said. "They think we're pests. Hey, talking about pests, where are the twins?"

"They're late," Bea said. "Maybe they won't show up. Two less angels won't make much difference."

"But they'll miss the cast party," Rebecca said.

"I won't miss them!" Bea said.

Margaret dodged the tag game as she crossed the room. "Have you seen the twins?" Bea asked her.

"They came in as the makeup lady finished with me," Margaret said. "They were carrying a box. Were we supposed to bring things for the party?"

Rebecca shook her head. "We didn't last year. The director ordered a huge cake with Clara and the Nutcracker on top. Maybe the twins brought favors, lollipops, or pins."

"They'd never do anything nice," Bea said. "Believe me. I see them in class every week."

Margaret had to leave for the opening scene, and the party children lined up near the stage entrance. "Quiet down, everyone," the stage manager said. "This is the last show. Make it your best."

The twins hurried into the room carrying the box that Margaret had mentioned. They set it on the floor in the corner. I bet they brought their own food for the party, Bea thought. They probably won't even share.

The orchestra started the overture. Bea pictured the dancers dressed in winter coats and hats, passing each other on the street and Drosselmeyer hurrying by carrying his present, a nutcracker, of course.

Next the party children went onstage for their scene. The music for their dance drifted backstage. Bea bowed to Rebecca and Rebecca curtsied. Keeping time with the music from the stage, they danced their own version of the party waltz.

They were interrupted when the stage manager stomped past them pulling Erin and Caitlin behind him, with their mystery box tucked under his arm. "Get the director fast," he ordered his assistant. "Sit here, you two, and don't move," he barked at the twins, plopping them onto a bench near the coatracks.

The twins sat side by side with their heads bowed. The stage manager paced back and forth in front of them. Soon the director hurried through the room. He was dressed in a fancy black suit, ready to celebrate. But instead of a happy smile, he wore a dark scowl on his face.

"You won't believe this," the stage manager sputtered. "I found these so-called angels in the wings next to Clara's bed. They'd already pulled down the covers. Take a look at this!" He opened the lid of the box. "Glue, shaving cream, paint, nail polish. One fine mess they'd planned. I caught them just in time."

The director poked through the contents of the box. "Stand up!" he ordered. Caitlin and Erin slowly rose from the bench. They kept their heads low, frightened by his anger. "What were you thinking? A stunt like this could ruin the whole performance."

"We were just playing a trick," Erin said, her voice quivering.

"A trick?" The director bellowed. "On whom?"

"On Margaret," Caitlin answered.

"Why would you do that to her?" the director asked. "It would have embarrassed her in front of the whole audience."

The twins shrugged. They wouldn't look up.

The director stood with his arms crossed. "In all the years I've been staging ballets, I've never seen a stunt like this before. This isn't silly or funny. It's mean—cruel, jealous, and mean."

He turned to the stage manager. "We'll manage with two less angels today. Keep these two right here until their parents arrive."

Turning back to the twins, he said, "You've danced your last ballet with this company, and if I have any say in it, you won't be welcome at ballet school either." The director turned sharply and left.

The cue for the polichinelles came soon. By the end of Mother Ginger's dance, the twins had disappeared. Bea cringed, imagining the scene in the director's office.

After all the bows and bouquets, the dancers turned in their costumes and gathered for the cast party. Bea, Rebecca, and Margaret sat on the floor eating cake and sipping soda. Bea and Rebecca took turns describing the twins' scheme.

Margaret put her hands on her cheeks, horrified. "Imagine if they hadn't been caught! The stage is so dim then and I have to hurry into my nightgown and get into the bed fast. I wouldn't have seen anything until it was too late. Yuck! Think of all that goo." She shuddered.

"What a pair of brats," Rebecca said.

"You mean *devils!*" Bea said.

"I hope I never see them again," Margaret said.

"The director said they probably won't be welcome at ballet school. And I'm glad," Bea said.

The girls pulled on their coats and hats, slung their ballet bags over their shoulders and climbed the stairs to the stage door for the last time this season. Rebecca waved good-bye and hurried off with her mother.

During the performance, snow had begun to fall. Big thick flakes drifted down from the sky. Bea tried to catch a snowflake on her tongue.

"You promised to take me skating when we finished the ballet," Margaret reminded Bea. "Let's go next week."

"That's right! We still have some vacation left. We can skate at the town rink or in Pete's backyard. Skating outside at night is the best," Bea said.

"But there aren't any sides to hold onto at Pete's skating rink," Margaret said.

"You won't need to hold on," Bea said. "You'll be skating in no time. I promise."

"Like this?" Margaret slid across the sidewalk on one foot.

Bea copied her, skidding on the snow. She hit an icy

patch and her feet slipped out and down she went, landing on her bottom. "Not like this!" she said, laughing.

Lying on her back, Bea swung her arms and legs in arcs to make an angel's wings and skirt. Margaret lay down beside her and made a second angel. They stood back up and brushed the snow from the back of each other's coat.

Bea drew halos above the angels' heads. "These angels won't play any nasty tricks."

"Don't be so sure," Margaret said with a grin. She drew horns and a tail on each.

"No way!" Bea said. She shuffled back and forth across the sidewalk. Margaret joined her in a slip-sliding dance. Together, they erased the angels completely.